FOR
Maria & Kitty

First published in Great Britain 1997
by Methuen Children's Books
an imprint of Reed International Books Ltd
Michelin House, 81 Fulham Road, London SW3 6RB
and Auckland, Melbourne, Singapore and Toronto

Text and illustrations copyright © Belinda Downes 1997
1 3 5 7 9 10 8 6 4 2

ISBN 0 416 19364 1

A CIP catalogue record for this title is
available from the British Library

Produced by Mandarin Offset Ltd
Printed and bound in China

Every Little Angel's Handbook

words & embroideries
by Belinda Downes

METHUEN

Angels are all around us at all times.
We may not see them, but they're there.
And they don't just sit around on clouds all day.
Angels have work to do, people to visit and
messages to deliver. They have rainbows to paint,
stars to polish and snow to make.

Little angels have to learn to fly, and sing,
and shoot arrows, and make angel cakes.
And most importantly, they have to learn to look
and behave like proper little angels.

If you are considering becoming a little angel,
read carefully and you will learn everything
you need to know.

Angel Tree

Gabriella
Guardian Angel

Angelica
Cookery Mistress

Gloria
Choir Mistress

Eric
Star Keeper

Mabel
Snow & Ice Maker

Bob
Special Effects Angel

Every little angel needs guidance. They must learn special skills for their
important work. The older, wiser angels are in charge of day-to-day activities
and teaching the younger angels.

Peter
Head Teacher

Beatrice
Star Catcher

Ariel
Flight Controller

John Francis
Special Effects Angel

Tabitha
Weather Angel

Valentino
Chief Cupid

Some are very serious and a little bit cross,
others are full of fun. But they are all very kind and understanding.
Here are some of the most important and hardworking angels.

Angel Style

Angels are very fussy about their appearance and they certainly don't all wear white.

Icing Sugar

Summer

Firebird

Rainbow

Traditional

Midnight

From the plain and humble traditional look to something for that special angelic occasion, angels can choose from their very own style catalogue. Even the most fashion conscious will find the perfect outfit.

Choosing accessories to match is just as easy.
Not all angels have dainty feet.
Eight out of ten guardian angels prefer sturdy boots in case they
have to help little devils mind their own business.

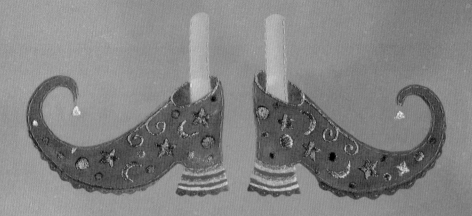

Extrovert
With good grip for tricky earth landings and
tinkling bells on the toes, these boots are perfect
for angels who like to be seen and heard.

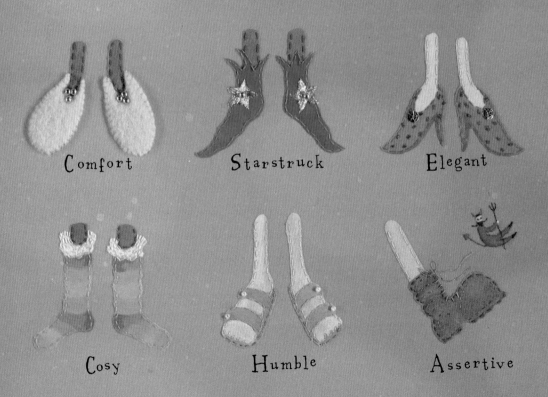

Comfort   Starstruck   Elegant

Cosy   Humble   Assertive

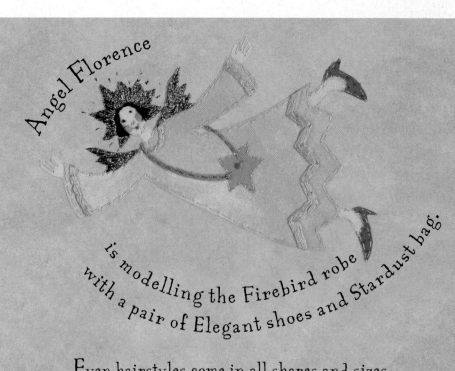

Angel Florence is modelling the Firebird robe with a pair of Elegant shoes and Stardust bag.

Even hairstyles come in all shapes and sizes.
Some are easy to manage but others,
such as Lightning, cause havoc in the heavens.

Romantic   Cupid Curl   Basic

Lightning   Crazy Curl   Roly Poly

Bags are useful for carrying stardust, angel dust,
wing spray, star polish and emergency supplies of vanishing powder,
even notebooks for those long lists of things to do and people to see.

Astral Purse   Stardust   Starburst   Exotic

Of course, every little angel needs wings and a halo.

Golden Cloud   Regal   Go-lightly

Sunlight   Earth   Dazzler

Large, small, plain, patterned, frosted, gold, silver or see-through,
the angel catalogue has them all. It could take an age to choose.

Angel Profile No.1: Eric

Eric works in the star department.
His robe of midnight blue allows him to fly unseen
through the starry night skies.
His soft curly-toed shoes are practical and easy-to-wear.
Stars need regular maintenance and must be
taken down, cleaned and put back in place before
anyone notices.

Eric and his friends polish stars with magic stardust
and fly around all night chasing shooting stars
and catching falling ones.
Dark glasses are useful when unexpected stars whizz by,
sparkling and fizzing with tails of bright lights.

Angel Profile No.2: Mabel

Mabel works for the snow and ice department.
It's cold work but her Fluffy Cloud robe keeps her warm.
The most difficult part of her job is cutting out snowflakes so that
each one has its own unique pattern.
Only the most patient angels are chosen to do this.

Angel Profile No.3: Angelica

Angelica Pudding is taking a cookery class.
Today, she is teaching cake-making so complete concentration is needed.
Cakes are Angelica's speciality. They are always light and fluffy and
taste delicious, if you can manage to catch one.

When Angelica isn't looking, the little angels
can be mischievous. They squirt icing at each other,
spill flour and throw cake mixture down to earth.
Teaching cookery is a messy business!

Angel Profile No.4: Gloria

Gloria, the choir mistress, needs a lot of patience.
(She used to make snowflakes.)
The little angels often sing wrong notes or even
completely different songs but Gloria always remains calm.
She taps her conductor's baton and off they go again.

Little angels need lots of practice if they are ever to reach heavenly
standards and sing at special angelic events.
This choir loves singing wedding marches,
Christmas carols and lullabies.

Flying Lessons

The problem with learning to fly is that little angels get over-excited and fly too far and too fast before they are ready. Flight Controller, Angel Ariel, tries to teach take-off, landing and perfect wing control before he allows any fancy flying.

Wings need constant care and repair. Patching up holes just won't do.

Sky dives and somersaults are too advanced for beginners but Mavis
likes to show off with a triple twist take-off. Oh dear, her wings are
much too delicate!

All day long expert angels stitch, glue, brush and restore tired wings.
Artist angels paint and decorate them to look good as new.

Weather Angels

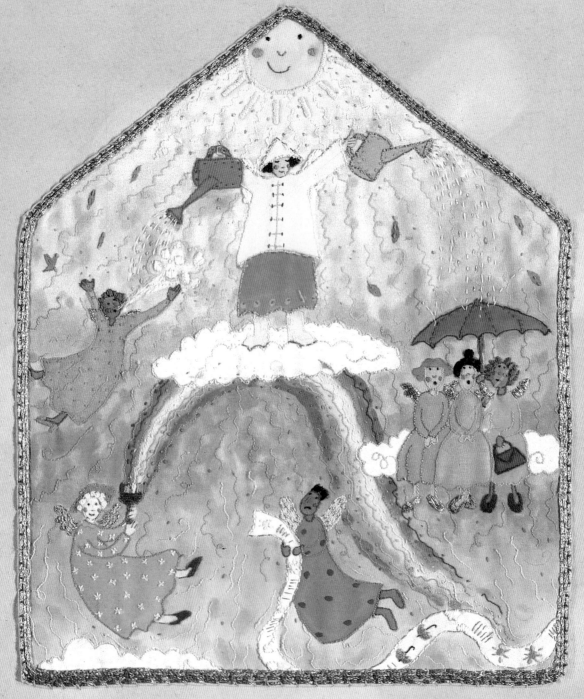

The weather is planned in advance but doesn't always turn out
as expected. Sometimes everything gets muddled, the angels get
confused and one minute it's raining and the next it's sunny.
Summer is best when angels flit and float on gentle breezes.
Clouds are cleared away to let the sun shine through.

Guardian angels make sure we don't get into trouble,
lose things or have accidents.
But little guardians also need looking after so Angel Gabriella stays
close by, watching over her busy little group. She wears a bright,
glittering star on her dress so that her angels can find her quickly
if they ever do get into trouble themselves!

Cupid Angels

Cupids are probably the laziest angels of all. They really enjoy lying around on clouds all day. Cupids have great fun making people all over the world fall in love. Angel Valentino has to remind them that it's a serious business. They should ensure that arrows don't go astray.

Special Effects

Angels Bob and John Francis are a good team when it comes to
organising special effects in the heavens. Red skies at night,
eclipses, comets and shooting stars are among their favourites.
They run the star department where Eric works. There he is, busy
polishing stars. Only angels who have passed their advanced flying
test can be taught to put stars in the sky.

As the world turns around and around, day becomes night and night becomes day. Angels are kept busy from dawn till dusk. Flying over the earth they have a great view of the world and as we sleep they wish us well and send us little messages in our dreams.